To Quinn & Spencer & Maddie,
i hope you love Tyrance
& he brings you lots
of joy. Hilary

Fantasic Forms Presents

Terrance The Trapezoid

Hilary and Drew McSherry

Illustrated by Drew McSherry

Archway Publishing books may be ordered through booksellers or by contacting:

Archway Publishing
1663 Liberty Drive
Bloomington, IN 47403
www.archwaypublishing.com
1-(888)-242-5904

ISBN: 978-1-4808-0131-8 (sc)
ISBN: 978-1-4808-0130-1 (e)

Printed in the United States of America

Archway Publishing rev. date: 8/29/2013

"Coming together is a beginning;
keeping together is progress;
working together is success."

-Henry Ford

To my parents, Jane and John Orzel, and my sister, Helen Orzel

To my parents Bill and Betsy McSherry

Fantasic Forms Presents

Terrance The Trapezoid

Hilary and Drew McSherry

Illustrated by Drew McSherry

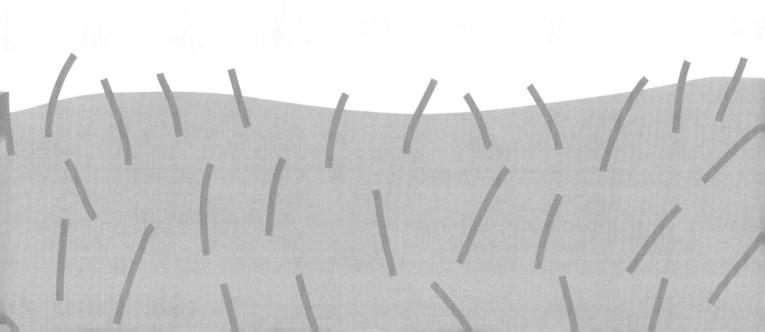

Terrance the Trapezoid often sat alone on a hill, watching other shapes play. He felt like he didn't fit in, so Terrance never joined in their games.

He wasn't like the other shapes. A circle, triangle, and square could be lots of different things, but not Terrance. He couldn't see anything that was made from a trapezoid.

Sammy the Circle could be an eyeball, a balloon, and even the sun.

Tammy the Triangle could be a tree, a tooth, and a beautiful dress.

**Sid the Square could be a pizza box,
a road sign, and a window.**

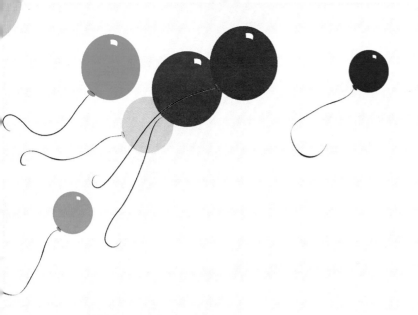

Terrance tried and tried to be like the other shapes,
but he didn't do a very good job.

One day, Tammy, Sammy, and Sid noticed that Terrance was sitting all alone. He had a big frown on his face. "Why do you look so sad?" asked Sid. Terrance mumbled, "It's because I don't fit in." The other shapes wanted to help. They had to show Terrance that something could be made from a trapezoid, but what?

Tammy, Sammy and Sid thought and thought. Finally, they had an idea!

"Terrance!" Sid said happily. "If we all work together, we can each be a different part of a whole new shape!" Terrance was very excited. They all came together and created......

A Boat.

A Bird.

An Aquarium.
And then...

They made a rocket ship and flew to the moon.

Terrance was such a happy shape because now he fit in.

Reader's guide: Discussion

Why did the other shapes decide to help Terrance?

How did Terrance feel when he tried to be like the other shapes and couldn't? How did he feel when the others included him?

Do you think that the bird in the story could fly to an island? Could Terrance go to the island all alone, without the other shapes?

Look around the room. What do you see that is a circle, a triangle, a square, and a trapezoid?

When have you worked together with other people? When did you try to include someone?

At the beginning of the story, did Terrance like being a Trapezoid? At the end, how do you think he felt about being a Trapezoid?

Activities

Create a picture of a complex shape like a boat, and trace the simple shapes inside of it. Have children find the simple shapes and color them various colors.

Create cut outs of different shapes. From the examples in the book, decide which complex shape the children should make: A boat, bird, aquarium, or rocket ship. Have them put the cut outs together to create that complex shape.

Suggestions for older readers

Look around the room. What do you see that could be made up of more than one shape?

Create cut outs of different shapes. Have children put the cutouts together to make their own complex shape. To vary the activity, have children work with just 2 shapes, 3 shapes, or include 2 or more of the same shape.

Compare and Contrast the attributes of Terrance and his friends. For example, how many sides and corners do they have?

Hilary McSherry

received a Bachelor of Arts degree in Music and a Bachelor of Arts degree in International Relations from the University of the Pacific. She also received a Master of Arts degree in International Policy from the Monterey Institute of International Studies. Her work as a writer, musician, teacher, and an agent of social change has taken her all over the world learning about people, culture, and creativity.

Drew McSherry

received a Bachelor of Arts degree in Graphic Design from Loyola Marymount University and a Master of Fine Arts degree in Children's Book Illustration from the Academy of Art University. He has worked as an illustrator, painter, and teacher, focusing on helping others reflect and nurturing creativity.

CPSIA information can be obtained
at www.ICGtesting.com
Printed in the USA
BVXC01n0518060314
346824BV00001BA/1